Conrad's Big Surprise!
The Adventures of Conrad

Written by HANNAH PERRY & CATHERINE PARK
Illustrated by HANNAH PERRY

Dedications

To all the wonderful families who visit
The Giggling Pig each year to celebrate their
birthdays. We are so grateful to be a
part of your memories.
- Hannah

To my children.
Never stop being creative.
- Catherine

It was a sunny morning in Honeysuckle Village and a very special day for one little chick. Conrad woke from a dreamy sleep and gave a big stretch, a little chirp and rubbed his eyes.

He had an exciting day ahead.

"It's my birthday, happy birthday to me!" Conrad sang out. Mimi was taking him to the Sweets and Treats bakery for a special treat. Conrad loved cupcakes, especially ones with sprinkles on.

There was a knock at the door. It was Mimi.
"Happy birthday Conrad," she said handing him a party hat and balloon.
"Let's go!" Conrad said dashing out the door.
Before he knew it, he was standing outside the bakery peering through the window at the treats on display.
"They sure look yummy, let's go in," said Mimi.

"Good morning" said a voice from behind the counter.

"Hello Billie," Conrad smiled.

"Mimi said I could choose my favorite cupcake for my birthday."

"Instead, why don't you help me make your favorite cupcake?" Billie suggested.

"Wow, I'd love that." Conrad was excited to learn how to bake.

They went into the kitchen and Conrad noticed all the ingredients were ready on the counter.

As he reached for a spoon Billie stopped him.

"Before we touch anything, we have to wash our hands," she explained.

"There are many things we need to do before baking."

Billie went over everything with Conrad and they were soon ready with clean hands and aprons tied. Conrad was eager to get started.

The recipe book was opened and Conrad took a quick glance over it. He thought how tricky it looked. There were lots of words and numbers and he wasn't really sure what it all meant.

But it was his birthday, and he really wanted to show Mimi he could do things on his own.

"Do you need help, you look a little confused?" asked Mimi.

"I'm fine," he answered feeling pretty confident.

Conrad looked at the flour. I will start with that he thought. Two and a half cups. But he looked at the measuring cups and none of them said two and a half.

He wasn't sure what to do.

"I know. I will use one cup twice," he mumbled to himself.

There were many words that Conrad couldn't read, so he glanced over to Billie and tried to copy her. He grabbed the spoon and started mixing everything together.

"I'm ready," he shouted.

"Great, now pour your mixture into these containers," said Billie pointing to the tray.

They turned the timer on and Billie placed
the trays in the oven.

"What do we do now?" Conrad asked.

"Every good baker cleans up their mess," Billie said
handing Conrad a cloth.

Conrad didn't feel so happy as he looked
at the big mess he'd made.

"This is hard work," he sighed.

"Being a baker takes a lot of patience and
practice Conrad," smiled Billie.

Before long the timer was beeping and
the cupcakes were ready to take out of the oven.

Billie put on her oven gloves and pulled them out.

"Oh no, my cupcakes!
They look awful," Conrad gasped.

"Did you follow my instructions?" Billie asked.

"No! I got confused and didn't
want to tell you I couldn't read
all the words," cried Conrad.

"Conrad please don't feel bad. I made many
mistakes when I was learning too.
That's how I got better at being a baker,"
Billie explained.

"Really?" Conrad wiped the tears
from his eyes.

"I am only a good baker today because I
never gave up.
So let's start again," Billie said.

Mimi helped Conrad to read the recipe and showed him which cups to use.

"1 cup + 1 cup + a half cup makes 2 and a half cups."

This time Mimi walked Conrad through the recipe step by step.

"I didn't realize I needed to do math when I baked," Conrad confessed.

"Now I see why it's important to listen and learn in school." They giggled and mixed all the ingredients together. Finally the cupcakes were ready to go in the oven.

Conrad felt worried that these cupcakes would come out wrong too.

Maybe he would never be a good baker.

He was so nervous but the timer went off and distracted him from his thoughts.

"Here we go," said Billie as she pulled out the tray from the oven.

"They look perfect Conrad, even better than mine!"

"Just like you said, practice makes perfect," Mimi said.

Conrad felt proud that he hadn't given up.

"Would you like to decorate your cupcakes?" Mimi asked.

"Yes, my favorite part," Conrad giggled.

"Thank you for helping me to be a baker. I didn't know how much hard work went into making cupcakes or how fun decorating could be. I feel like an artist."

"What did you learn today?" Mimi asked Conrad.

"I learned that baking is harder than I thought and you need to read and do math," Conrad replied as he reached for a cupcake.

"Before you eat that - I have one more surprise for you." Mimi led the way back into the bakery.

There, in the bakery were all Conrad's friends from Honeysuckle Village holding balloons and gifts ready to celebrate his special day. "Happy birthday to you..." they all began to sing. "This is the best birthday ever," beamed Conrad. Conrad blew out his candle and made his birthday wish...

What do you think it was?

The End.

Hannah Perry and Catherine Park first met in 1999 in the USA. They were both nannies and after spending a short time together decided to be best friends forever. They have big plans of working together in the future - so keep your eyes open and see what comes next!

The Giggling Pig currently has four art and party studio locations in Connecticut. One in Shelton ,Bethel, Seymour and Milford. Just like the stories, all studios encourage kindness and friendship, while enriching the lives of many families in Connecticut, New York and beyond.

You can learn more about our programs and visit our shop at www.thegigglingpig.com

Printed in Great Britain
by Amazon

12493483R00018